meg rosoff

moose baby

Barrington Stoke

First published in 2013 in Great Britain by
Barrington Stoke Ltd
18 Walker Street, Edinburgh, EH3 7LP

Adapted from a story previously published as
Vamoose!, Puffin, 2010

www.barringtonstoke.co.uk

ISBN: 978-1-78112-197-9

Printed in China by Leo

To Miss Kristina Gillett of Laycock School,
best nursery teacher ever

chapter 1

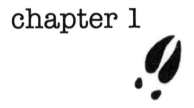

The midwife gave me the evil eye.

"Mothers your age often don't bond well," she said. Then she added, like it hurt her to say it, "It will come."

My age? Jeez. It's not like I was twelve or something.

She and I had spent the last ten minutes glaring at each other, but I couldn't help admiring the way she held my baby. She hugged him close to her great big bazooms and looked into his big velvet eyes. Her smile (at him) appeared to be real. Which was a plus.

"Who's a dear little sweet thing?" she purred. "Who's a beautiful big moosie boy?" My baby gazed back at her with love, his eyes wide open. "Look at those eyelashes!" she said. She turned to me again. "Well, he may not be what you expected, but he is a beauty."

"I wish you'd tell that to my mum," I said. "She refuses to look at him." I squinted and searched for the beauty in the curve of his nose, his little baby nostrils. "I guess she has a point. He is kind of hairy."

"Don't you mind about that, now," the midwife said. "Just look at his lovely wee hooves."

She held out one tiny foot, shiny and ebony black. It was cute. I closed my eyes, still pretty numb and sick from the C-section. And a little dizzy from getting used to things. I mean, how exactly had this happened? The 20-week scan had looked perfectly normal.

"It's a late development in some pregnancies," the consultant said. "We often fail to pick it up on the blood test." He spoke in an 'I'm-SO-much-more-important-than-you' voice, slithering out of any and all blame at the same time. "We've had a small cluster of non-homo-sapien births this year," he told me. "They're not common. Mainly moose. No one knows why."

I squeezed my eyes into slits and all of a sudden I realised that he wasn't a doctor at all – he was a zombie! Heh heh. Of course he hadn't looked so smug when Mum threatened to sue the hospital over my non-homo-sapien birth. He'd looked even sicker than I felt.

"Something to help you sleep?" the zombie-doctor asked. His eyebrow was elevated a little, as if to suggest that he'd accept if it were *his* child. "We'll send the social worker round first thing in the morning," he said. "In the meantime, try to get some rest. It won't all look so bad in daylight."

Did he mean the situation, or my baby?

I didn't think either was going to look a whole lot better in the clear light of day.

chapter 2

"Well, I guess we can't call him Imogen."
Nick stared at the furry creature in the
cot. I could understand his disappointment.
We'd both been convinced we were having a
girl. And a human being.

"What do you suggest? We have to call
him something. Lucas doesn't seem right
either."

"Bullwinkle?"

"Very funny, Nick."

But when I turned back to him, he looked
glum. "What on earth am I going to tell my
parents?"

"Yeah, that's our biggest worry," I
said. "Give me the phone, I'll break the
news." I lifted an imaginary phone to my
ear. "'Hello, Anthony? Camille? Your son's
girlfriend's given birth to a bouncing baby

moose. Twenty three pounds – by C-section, in case you were wondering. Yeah, *that's* why I got so fat. Big floppy ears and lots of hair. Mother and son doing well. Father not so good.'"

I don't know what I expected when I had finished my performance, but Nick seemed really stricken. I sighed. "Look, Nick, they'll cope. It's us I'm worried about." I reached over and took his hand. In the plastic cot beside me, Baby Moose Pearson slept in a pale blue hospital blanket. None of the cute Babygros I'd bought fitted. He muttered and squeaked in his sleep. His floppy nose wrinkled and unwrinkled.

Tears filled Nick's eyes. "My son."

"What about 'Moe'?" I asked.

"Moe Moose?" Nick stared at me. "Have you ever been in a school playground?"

"Moe Pearson, actually." But I took his point.

My phone rang and Nick answered. "It's your mum," he said.

I shook my head.

"She's asleep," he lied to Mum. Then he listened for a minute. "OK, I'll tell her." He rang off and handed back my phone. "She says she loves you no matter what, but that you're really pushing it this time."

"Did you tell her it wasn't my idea to give birth to a moose?"

Nick shrugged. "She probably knows that."

At last Nick seemed to remember that this hadn't been a great day for me either. "My poor Jess." He sat on the edge of the bed and gave me a clumsy hug, trying to avoid the drip. "What a time you've had."

Too right. My eyes drooped as a new nurse swept through the door, a large woman in a stripy uniform.

"Baby Boy Pearson?" the nurse said. Her accent was Irish. "I've got him on my list for a special feed." She peered into the plastic cot and her face split into a huge grin. "Well, well, well. Will you look at that little thing?" She lifted him out of the cot, laid him in the curve of her arm and gave a comedy groan at the weight of him. "Excuse me, not so little. Who's a sweet boy then? Who's the sweetest, handsomest boy?"

I tried to see him through her eyes. He *was* cute. He looked like one of those big cuddly toys you might buy at Hamley's. The sort of thing you'd stick at the end of a proper baby's cot. I closed my eyes.

"Look, Jess, I think I'd better get going."

I nodded. So tired.

"Night, night." Nick seemed unwilling to let go of my hand. "I'll be back first thing."

"Uh-huh."

Seventeen. Pregnant. And now this.
Sleep was definitely my best option.

chapter 3

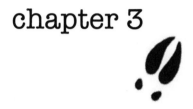

"What about Rudolph?"

"I see you've got your sense of humour back." I was in a chair with my baby against my chest, the way the Breast-Feeding Advisor had shown me. But it was no good. He showed no desire to latch on, despite having more than enough lip for the job. Nick put him back in his cot.

"So ... nothing's changed?" he asked.

His question was totally pathetic. What had he been expecting? A letter from the hospital? "Sorry, folks, we made a mistake. In fact, your baby belongs to a large female elk who checked in around the same time you did."

"Nope." I indicated the bundle. "Nurse said he drank like a sailor in the night."

"That's my boy." For a second, Nick looked quite proud.

"But he isn't farting and begging for aspirin this morning, so maybe he takes after someone else."

"Rudolph. Rudy." Nick tried the name out. He giggled. "Reminds me of a really fit guy in tights doing ballet, with a great big bulging – "

"Stop that image right now, before it sticks. Maybe we should go back to one of the names we thought of before."

"Oh no, please. Not Lucas."

"So …?"

"How 'bout Mickey? *Mickey Moose?*" Nick doubled over laughing.

I'd have happily ripped out every one of my eighteen stitches to punch him, but he was saved by the arrival of Mum. She was followed by Marion Staines, Medical Social Worker.

"You must be Jessica Pearson?" the Social Worker said. I could see her running down a checklist in her head:

Teen mother.

Piercings.

Tattoos.

Baby blues.

Failing to bond.

Poor parenting skills.

I didn't have to guess at Mum's checklist:

Kill daughter's boyfriend.

Kill daughter.

Send moose baby to zoo.

"Hi, Mum."

"Hello, sweetheart. Did you get some sleep?" I could tell Mum had made up her mind to be nice in front of the Social Worker.

"Pills." I held up the little packet they'd left me.

"*Now* you're taking pills?"

I walked into that one.

My eyes met Miss Staines' and she looked away. I bet she never had to deal with three generations of a moose family before.

"Well ..." she began, a little unsure. "So this is baby ...?"

"Rudolph," I said. Out of the corner of my eye, I saw Nick wince.

"Would you like to hold him, Mum?"

'Don't call me "Mum",' I thought. There was only one mum in this room and that was the one glaring at me from behind the world's fakest smile. And anyway, the short answer was no, I didn't want to hold him. I wanted to hold a baby like everyone else had. Or better yet, a box of Krispy Kremes.

Miss Staines put down her notebook and lifted the baby out of the cot, grunting a bit.

"There you go, Mum," she said, and handed him to me. "Isn't he sweet?" She smiled a broad, patronising smile.

I glared at her as I took him. "Do you have kids, Ms ..." I peered at her name-tag. "Staines?"

She smiled her best hippy smile. "I've always surrounded myself with little ones."

Little ones? I nearly gagged. "Did any of those little ones have hooves?" I lifted one of Rudolph's skinny moose legs and waved it at her.

"No." She glanced towards heaven. "But I'd have loved them just the same if they had."

"MUM!"

Mum took her by the arm and led her over to the door. "Jess can be a bit moody," she whispered, loud enough for me to hear.

21

"Get her out of here!" I wanted to kill them both.

Mum gave me a look that said, *Well, this is just the sort of situation you get into when you don't listen to me about having sex and are too much of an irresponsible know-all to remember to use contraception properly. To be frank, it serves you right – it wasn't me who suggested you get knocked up by that useless posh boy.*

My mum's got a very expressive face.

Then she sighed and said she was going for a cappuccino and did anyone want one? But by the time I said yeah, I could murder a double mocha latte, she'd scarpered.

"Miss Pearson – " The social worker was creeping back into the ring for another round.

"Jess," I said. "My name is Jess."

"Miss Pearson, is this ... this person the baby's father?" I could tell she wanted to say 'boy'.

It was clear that Nick hated her as much as I did, which made me remember why I loved him. But only for a moment.

"*She* says I'm the father," he said, and pointed a finger at me. "But I think she's lying. There are all sorts in my line – Orthodox Jews, Rastafarians, pygmies. But not a single moose." He crossed his arms.

Over to me.

I sniggered. "Don't look at me. High Church top to bottom. Nothing suspect anywhere in *my* family."

At last poor Miss Staines was getting flustered. I flashed Nick a smile – score! Miss Staines made a note on her pad and pushed a strand of mousy hair behind one ear.

"I'd like us to try a little bonding game," she said. "Mum, hold Baby on your lap. Dad, stand behind her and to the left, and look over her shoulder at your baby. I want you both to mirror each of his little movements and expressions." She took a step back and tried out her saintly smile. It came out crooked.

Nick and I stared hard at our baby. The baby stiffened, and a far-away look came into his eye. And then there was a kind of trumpeting phlapppppppp noise followed by the rich forest smell of ... of moose poo.

I glared at her. "I'm not mirroring that."

"Motherhood is full of Unique Challenges," she said, in her saint voice. "We'll just change Baby's nappy and start again. Try to keep eye contact the whole time."

I tried, but failed. Scraping a bucket of poo off a furry animal is enough of a Unique Challenge with both eyes on the job.

When at last Miss Staines left, she looked utterly done in. Nick and I, on the other hand, had cheered up quite a bit.

"We might have to make it work," he said. "Just to ward off social workers."

I giggled and made a cross with my fingers. "Like vampires."

Nick picked Moosie up out of the cot, lifted him to eye-level and swapped his own voice for his dad's. "Of course we'll have to put him down for Eton."

I sighed and thought of the cute little sheepskin baby booties Jasmine had bought on the school trip to Wales – only two, and totally the wrong shape.

The Unique Challenges were coming thick and fast.

chapter 4

Moosie was six weeks old when we were invited to meet other members of our animal-baby 'cluster group'. The first meeting was in Richmond, in a big posh house owned by a lawyer and her husband. There were seven parents at the meeting – three couples and me. They were all about Mum's age, which freaked me out from the start. I was already seething with anger that Nick wasn't there. Liverpool were playing, but he promised he'd come next time.

Yeah.

Our baby had been up and walking more or less from birth, sticking his funny nose into everything. I can't say I was getting used to being a mother, but I was doing what was needed to keep both of us alive and out of jail.

I fed him special milk topped up with fresh grass and twigs, and he was already the size of a small pony. At local baby groups the mums looked down their noses at him almost as much as they did at me. But the other babies adored him. They squeaked with joy when he arrived, and rushed to chew on his tail or grab his floppy ears. They giggled for hours at the noises that came from his moosey bottom. He was such a sweet furry thing, gentle and friendly and shy, and after a while the nasty comments from other parents tailed off. About him, at least. They were still dying to say, "of course *that's* what comes of having kids too young" to me.

Mum wouldn't admit it but I could tell she liked having him around, and after I screamed four hundred million times that I WOULD NOT put him up for adoption, she backed off. She comes on like a dragon, my mum, but underneath she's a … dragon. About ten thousand miles under that, she's mush.

It was Mum's idea that I should bond with other animal-baby parents. It seems there'd been a piece in the paper, and there was even an organisation – Parents Of Non-homo-sapien Young, or PONY. But you don't notice that kind of stuff if all you read is music mags. Mum left the *Guardian* open on the kitchen table to a page with a picture of a cheery couple and their bouncing moose baby. He was all decked out in designer baby clothes, so he just seemed like part of a cool new trend. When I refused to read it, she sent an email to the address at the bottom of the article herself. She got an answer back right away – an invite for me 'and my husband or partner' to go along to the next month's PONY meeting.

Mum came with us right to the door so I couldn't escape. I recognised the woman who opened it from the newspaper photo. She had a big boy moose and a pretty little blonde toddler tugging at her skirt. "Come in, come in," she said, looking from Mum to Moosie to me, desperate to figure out how we were all connected. But Mum skedaddled, which left the woman more puzzled than ever. I stood on the doorstep like that painting of *The Scream*.

The woman didn't seem to notice. "Hello!" she said. "I'm Alice. Marc is somewhere, and this is Sebastian," she waved at the moose baby and his non-moose sister, "and Molly."

"This is Lucas Imogen Rudolph," I told her, "but we call him Moosie."

Alice showed us into a big living-room with white sofas and a huge Italian coffee table. She started to offer me wine, but then thought better of it and steered me to the apple juice instead. Moosie stood politely watching a game of Buckaroo, waiting for a chance to play. One or two parents commented on what good manners he had.

"Of course he's still young," Alice said with a sigh. "Sebastian was such a love at his age."

What did she mean? Under his stupid designer clothes, Sebastian still seemed like a sweet little moose.

The large woman sitting next to me told me her name was Mona. When Alice disappeared into the kitchen, she said in a low voice, "Sebastian gored their Labrador. To death."

Whoa.

"Of course," Mona went on, with a fake smile, "some non-homo-sapien babies are more difficult than others. Moose babies can be particularly difficult."

To prove her point, she called her baby and he waddled over. "This is Viktor, our youngest. We haven't had a minute's trouble with him." She lowered her voice. "I think it's because we treat him just the same as our other children. We don't want Viktor ever to feel different, do we, Craig dear?"

"I'm not even sure he realises he *is* different." 'Craig dear' chuckled.

Viktor was an emu.

Mona and Craig were freaks.

The next family, Ari and Sarah Bloom, had three little boys and Rivka, a little girl moose. The boys had long curly locks over their ears and skull-caps. Rivka wore a ruffled yellow dress, with little yellow stripy booties on her feet. I wondered if moose was even kosher.

Moosie and Rivka looked quite happy playing together until Moosie pulled Rivka's dress off with his teeth. Sarah snatched her daughter out of harm's way.

"See what I mean?" Mona hissed. "You'll have to keep an eye on him when he's in rut."

My baby? In rut? I was going to be sick.

Marc stood up and tapped on his wine glass. "Now that we're all here," he said, "perhaps we should open the meeting." He turned to Alice.

Alice stood up and smiled. "First of all, a warm welcome to our new members. As I'm sure you're already finding out, a non-homo-sapien child can be a unique challenge for any family, and a unique joy too."

Oh God, not another Unique Challenge.

Alice paused, her face stern. "It is only by opening our arms to life's wonderful gifts that each of us can begin to fulfil our special destinies."

'Hoo boy,' I thought, missing Nick. I peered around the room in the hope I'd spot a soulmate – someone, anyone, doing eye rolling or lip curling. But it was clear I was the only one who heard words like 'wonderful gifts' and 'special destinies' and wanted to barf.

"The point is," Alice went on, "that together we must fight for our children to be treated as equals."

"No special schools?" Craig asked. He looked worried.

"No, no, no," Alice said. "When the time comes, Sebastian will attend a mainstream school, perhaps with a support worker to help with some of the challenges – "

Sarah raised her hand. "What sort of challenges are you thinking of?"

"I'm glad you asked." Alice pulled out a neat typed sheet of A4 paper and began to read a list. "We thought he might have trouble with:

Anger management

Arithmetic

Art

Batting at games

Bonding with other children

Carol singing

Calculus

Chemistry...

It went on.

... Handwriting ... Homework ..."

I drifted into a coma, but no one seemed to notice.

"... Long division ... Logarithms ..." She droned on and on until she reached 'Zoo Visits', which seemed quite fitting. After that there was a stunned silence. Moosie grabbed the moment by squatting and emitting a great squirting stream of green poo on to Alice and Marc's fluffy white sheepskin rug. He was a child after my own heart when it came to attention-seeking behaviour.

Oops. Had Alice mentioned potty training while I dozed? I swept my cheerful moose out of the room, muttering something about him having a funny tummy. Rivka's mother started to retch.

"Let's blow this joint, Moosie," I whispered into his furry ear. "Dunno about you, but I'm not ready to sign up for the WI."

Mum was waiting for us around the corner at Starbucks. The ride home was a little on the silent side.

chapter 5

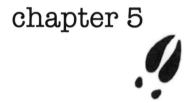

I had hoped to go back to school when my baby was six months old, but things didn't go to plan. For one thing, try finding a nursery or a child-minder who'll take a moose. And Mum wasn't quitting her job to take care of my baby – she'd made that clear when I first told her I was pregnant. I didn't blame her. Being a Human Resources Manager for The Most Boring Bank in The World Ltd was probably way more fun than playing with a moose baby all day.

In any case, Moosie was getting to be a real handful. By four months he tipped the scales at 85 kilos. He hurtled round the house in a gallop that shook the floors, knocked glasses off shelves and got all the lamps swinging. He loved it when I shouted, "Hi ho, Moosie, and away!" but after a while it looked like he might bring down the place, so I stopped.

His toilet habits were another problem. Nick came over after college every day and trained him to go in the garden, but for some reason I found this depressing. It was worst when people came to visit and right when I was showing them how cute he was playing with his toy rabbit, he'd leap to his feet with a bellow and head out the back door for a poo. It kind of trashed the subtle message I was working on, that he was a perfectly normal baby who just happened to be a moose.

Having a moose baby can tell you all sorts of things you might not have suspected about the grandparents. For all her hard line that if I was old enough to get pregnant, I was old enough to bring up my own baby, Mum began to show signs of surrender. She knitted little Bambi-sized blankets and beanie hats in the shape of strawberries. Moosie adored her, and every time she came home from work he did a special lolloping dance of joy that made the plaster fall off the ceiling. This was obviously my fault, cos she never seemed to blame Moosie for anything.

She started coming home early from the office to babysit and watch wildlife films with him. They cuddled up in bed together and ate popcorn, which was what she and I always used to do together when I was little.

"Who's Grandma's best little moose?" Mum would ask, and Moosie would shoot me little smug looks that seemed to say, "well, it sure as heck ain't you". I mean, is it normal to be snubbed by your own baby?

She read him *The Little Prince*, and *Mother Moose* – sorry, *Goose*. She tucked him into bed at night with "Rock-a-Bye Baby", and his great big moosey eyes would begin to droop with the first stages of sleep. Sometimes I'd hang around in the doorway feeling annoyed at how cute they were together, but basically I was pleased they liked each other. It made my life easier, for one thing.

One Saturday afternoon as Moosie lay snoring on the compost heap in the garden, I sat down next to Mum in the kitchen. "I really am thankful for everything you do for Moosie," I said. Which was true. And also I was hoping to go to Glastonbury, which would mean I'd need Mum to babysit.

She took her specs off.

"Well, of course I do things for him," she said. "He's my only grandson. And haven't you noticed? He has my legs."

"Be honest, Mum," I said. "Weren't you just a little disappointed when he was born?"

She fixed me with her strong, wise gaze. "Perhaps, just for a moment I was. But I knew I would grow to love him, just as I grew to love you and your sister."

Grew to love us? A little odd, but ... I shrugged.

My sister's twenty-four and lives in Australia. She was really nice when she heard I was pregnant – she didn't lord it over me or act all cross. She has a little girl of her own and she was excited when she heard Moosie was a boy. There was a long silence after we emailed the baby pictures, though. I think maybe she thought "moose" was some kind of fond nickname.

Nick's family weren't easy to win over either. His mum burst into tears more or less any time anyone said Moosie's name. I tried not to take it personally. She'd had her heart set on a Head Girl from Cheltenham Ladies College for Nick, not a 17-year-old DJ he'd met at a rave. It was clear they thought I'd only got pregnant to ruin Nick's prospects of ever getting season tickets to the opera at Glyndebourne or whatever it is posh people do. So they didn't exactly welcome Moosie with open arms, but Nick insisted on bringing him to their house to stay some weekends so they could all learn to love each other.

Once or twice Nick caught his mum trying to teach Moosie how to use a fish-knife. He thought that was a great sign, but really the problems went deeper. Nick made out his parents didn't care that they'd never be able to take Moosie to a garden party at Buckingham Palace, but when little silver teething rings and lace christening robes started arriving in the post from the relatives. I suspected they hadn't sent pictures with the birth announcement.

As for me – well, I loved Moosie. Of course I did. But I was also still reeling from having a baby who stood five foot tall, had fleas, and needed to have a special concrete floor put in to his playroom. Let's face it. I'd never really thought about having a toddler who chewed his cud.

"Where's my boy?" Nick would shout when he came in the door after school. And Moosie would slide head-first down the hall and dance a sort of ecstatic moose pogo. Nick got used to being in plaster – Moosie's wild welcomes each evening broke one of his arms, cracked his cheekbone and fractured three bones in his foot. They knew us at A & E now, and I got the feeling they thought I was one of those psycho pit bull girlfriends, all nice one minute and woo-woo tear-your-throat-out the next. Just because I had one small tattoo and a few eyebrow piercings. We never told them it was Moosie who was doing the damage in case social services got involved and took Nick away.

I admit I wondered whether Nick would ever look at me again in that lovesick way he did way back when we first met. But most of the time I was either too busy or too tired to think about it much.

Sometimes, late at night, Nick and I would stand together and gaze down at our son as he lay snoring away in his sagging bed – *my* sagging bed actually. When Nick went home I'd drag a duvet on to the sofa and lie there wondering how I'd ended up on this particular winding road of life. I'm not saying it was a bad road exactly, it just wasn't the one I'd been expecting.

chapter 6

Hanging around with your baby at home is completely different from having to send him to school. It's the difference between just being some kid with a baby and then all of a sudden being a Parent with a capital P. On the morning Nick and I took Moosie to my old primary school for the first time, it felt like a whole new chapter in our lives.

Most parents have three or four years to get used to the idea of their kid going to school. But at the rate Moosie was growing, we had to enrol him in nursery at just eight months. It totally weirded me out that my old nursery teacher, Miss Gillett, was still there. So I just tried to concentrate on Moosie, who was smart and proud in his new school uniform. Nick and I were both more nervous than he was.

"His socks are weird," Nick hissed at me. "Everyone's going to make fun of the way he looks."

"They're tube socks, for God's sake," I hissed back. "They're the only ones that fit."

"And that polo shirt's all bunched up at his armpits."

"Hey, Nick, I'm a DJ, not Stella McCartney. I did my best."

Nick bit his nail. "It's the little things that lead to bullying, you know. The wrong shirt, or bad football boots."

Or antlers. Duh.

Miss Gillett, to give her credit, didn't make any of the jokes she might have made. The one thing she did do was to look at me and say, "I didn't expect to see you back in my classroom *quite* so soon."

Me neither, to tell the truth. I shrugged. "This is Moosie."

I guess nursery teachers are trained not to throw up their hands in shock no matter what walks through the door. Miss Gillett didn't blink. Our little moose was given his own coat-hook with LUCAS written above it in big block letters, and Miss Gillett took a Polaroid photo of him to stick on the class board.

Nick watched as a tiny Nigerian girl walked up to Moosie. She had a shy smile and perfect cornrows in her hair. "Hello," she said, and clambered up on to the top of a bookcase to get closer to our son's eye-level. "I'm Kiki."

Moosie lowered his long velvet snout and snuffled in her ear. Kiki giggled, and Nick smiled at me. First day of school and already our son was friends with the coolest girl in the class. For one brief moment, we were both filled with hope. Even Moosie's toilet issues didn't freak out Miss Gillett. "We'll just let him out two or three times each morning," she said, with a no-nonsense smile. "He can do his business in the wildlife garden. Not every child has the same needs."

We were so happy.

But it didn't last. Within a week, the complaints started to stream in. There were crushed toes and bruises on the playground. One parent reported that our son had developed a habit of taking over the pirate ship in the play area, and that he would bellow at anyone who tried to get in to play. It was my private opinion that Kiki was egging Moosie on, but of course it was impossible to prove that.

Things came to a head when Kiki's mum picked her up early from school one day. The report we were given later said that Moosie had leapt to his feet, charged at her with a great roar, and pinned her up against the wall. She said that he had behaved "in a terrifying and aggressive manner".

"That's absurd," Nick fumed. "I'm sure it was just high spirits."

We were called to a meeting at school to decide what to do about Moosie. The committee took one look at him and made up their minds. The fact that he now weighed more than 100 kilos convinced them that he didn't belong in a nursery class.

"But he's just a baby," Nick pleaded.

Moosie pawed the floor and several members of the committee looked frightened.

Miss Gillett said she was sorry to see him go. "Perhaps you could bring him back when some of the other children have caught up with him in size," she said. But in our hearts, we knew it would never happen.

Nick raged about how unfair the system was. "Look at him!" he said. "He's a perfect, happy kid. Just cause he's a little bit different, they go all 'I'm afraid we'll have to exclude him from school'. They were set against him from the start."

"He's a moose, Nicky."

"I *know* he's a moose. But that doesn't mean he's some kind of freak."

It touched my heart to hear Nick defend Moosie, but I had to keep things real. "Actually, I think it does."

He sighed. "You know what I mean."

I did. I took his hand and, with a deep breath, I came out with what was on my mind. "Has it ever occurred to you that maybe ..." I paused. After all this time could I bring myself to say it? "Has it ever occurred to you that maybe Moosie might be happier somewhere else?"

For an instant Nick perked up. "You mean boarding school?"

"I was thinking more like ... Canada?"

He pulled away, angry. "Never."

With a single word, the subject was closed.

So we got Moosie on the special needs register and had him tested for dyslexia and dyspraxia. We fought for speech therapists and reading tutors, but in the end we had to accept that every person involved in his education reached the same conclusion. Moosie's poor language skills and lack of an opposable thumb were holding him back.

Nick's parents had a friend with a cousin in Cambridge who was an expert in hand surgery. Over Pimm's and strawberries at a party in Wimbledon, they booked an appointment for him to see Moosie and give his opinion. We sat in his plush offices in Harley Street and read from a folder that told us he'd performed successful surgeries to re-build the thumbs of a number of accident victims and Hollywood stars. It was a simple matter, he explained. He took skin from the upper arm, implanted artificial ligaments, pulled nerves down into the new thumb-shaped bit and hoped for the best. He warned us that it didn't work every time, and he'd never tried it on a hoof.

It sounded horrible. Nick wanted to try it; I didn't. I couldn't bear to see Moosie turned into Frankenstein's monster, cut and scraped and shaped into something he wasn't. Next thing I knew we'd be talking about a nose job, or getting his ears tucked up to make him that little bit more like the other kids. The thought made me crazy.

"No." I was determined.

"What do you mean, 'no'?"

"Just, no. I don't want him to go through all that pain when it's not going to work anyway. He's different. There's no point pretending he's not."

"But he could learn to hold a pen, or write poetry. He could play piano, or clarinet. How can you justify shutting off the entire world of the arts to him?"

Every once in a while, Nick sounds like a total tit. It's not his fault though. If you met his parents you'd understand.

"Nick," I sighed, tired of the conversation, "he's a moose. Moose don't play the clarinet." I hated being the negative one all the time, but Nick's fantasy of his son in the wind section of the London Symphony Orchestra was a little on the disturbing side as well.

chapter 7

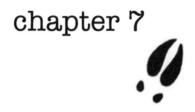

Moose children begin to show signs that puberty is on the way between the ages of two and three. They will go through a huge growth spurt, will develop a strong musty smell, and may become moody and difficult. Some parents are upset by the beginning of the first rutting season, which is marked by a constant loud croaking groan in boys.

So You Have a Moose Baby!
By Ann and Arnold Cooper, 4th edition

Our little Moosie was growing up.

At two years old he'd spend hours staring out the window with a sad, far-away look in his huge brown eyes. I had to ask myself more and more often if we were failing him. Home school gave his brain the exercise it needed, but what about his soul? Didn't he need a home where the buffalo roamed, and the deer and the antelope played? I was sure such a place existed. Canada still seemed the most likely option, but I'd looked into Norway, too. And Kamchatka.

Moosie now weighed 200 kilos and the facts of life were as follows: he was a boy moose. He needed a girl moose. For rutting. End of story.

I wasn't completely without pity. I knew a lot of teenagers who felt the same way.

Nick and I still saw each other and he was a good father to Moosie, but he was going off to university soon and I wasn't all that hopeful about us staying together. He said he still loved me, but everything he'd fallen in love with had changed – the fact that I was the coolest person he'd ever met, by a factor of a hundred billion, for example. I still kept up with new bands when I could, but late nights just wrecked me these days. OK, so I hadn't quite become one of those mothers who slopes off to the corner shop in her slippers for fags. But I could understand how a person might be tempted.

Day after day, the terrible noise of a growing moose in rut filled our little area of south London. Moosie dug a rutting pit in the garden, peed in it five times a day, and splashed the muddy pee all over his body. He thought it made him smell hot. I admired his confidence, but it didn't really work. For one thing, there weren't many girl moose in our local area. For another, there were the neighbours. We tried to explain time and again, but after a while it seemed simpler just to stop answering the phone. I sat with Moosie for hours and tried to distract him with Sudoku, board games and craft activities. But only old repeats on Wildlife TV interested him – he'd watch for hours in the hope of some brief glimpse of a naked girl moose. My son was turning into a moody, sulky teenager. Mum said I'd been exactly the same. Still was.

I couldn't cope. My GP sent me to someone with experience in depressed teenagers. I found myself in a little office at our local mental health unit, talking to a middle-aged man. He offered me a seat and once I started talking I couldn't stop.

"Are you angry with your son," he asked at last, "for making your life so complicated?"

Angry? Yes, maybe I was. I was also angry at him for destroying most of the furniture in the house and for filling every room with the stink of moose rut and great handfuls of flea-ridden hair. I was angry with him for smelling like a dead fox, and for making that horrible noise all the time. I was angry at the fact that he thought about sex night and day, that he refused to pay attention to his school-work, that he left great holes in the floor where he stamped his huge hooves ...

But most of all, I was bloody pissed off that he was going through his teenage years at the same time I was.

I began to sob. "I love Moosie," I gasped, "I love him. But he's *such a nightmare to live with.*"

"I have no doubt you love him," the therapist said. "I don't think love is the issue here. It won't change the way things are."

I knew something about the way things were. They were bad.

"What am I going to do?" I asked. I wiped my eyes and blew my nose.

"Well," he said, "whatever you choose, we'll support you. But only you can decide what's best for both of you."

I walked home, deep in thought.

Moosie began to sneak off to London Zoo at night to trumpet his frustration to the camels and llamas. There were no female moose at the zoo, but the smell of giraffes and bison drove him mad with desire.

The regular 5 a.m. call from the zoo keeper woke Nick, who staggered up to Camden with a leash and a bucket of Mars bars. When Moosie arrived home, I tried to stroke his head and rub his back, but he shook me off and stormed off to his room. Nick sighed, and asked if I would rub his back instead.

"This isn't working," he said at last.

"I'm sorry, but you have a lot of tension in your neck."

"I don't mean the massage," he said. "I mean the family."

For a moment I held my breath.

"Maybe ... we need to think about Canada again."

I breathed out. "Are you sure, Nick? Are you absolutely 100% sure?"

He nodded and we clung together, our faces wet with tears. The time had come.

chapter 8

I booked tickets for the three of us.
Moosie went in first class for the leg-room.
Nick and I were in economy. Nick's parents
paid for the tickets. They were so keen on
the plan that I nearly backed out.

Moosie loved the champagne and the
wide choice of nature programmes, but Nick
and I didn't even bother with the films. I
gazed out at the sun on the clouds and
thought of the way my baby had snuggled
into my arms and made me love him, the
way he always put his little moosie snout on
my shoulder and snuffled softly into my ear.

To any outsider, we were just a normal
family setting off on a normal camping
holiday to Desolation Bay ... with two return
tickets and one single. Nick squeezed my
hand and I let my head droop onto his
shoulder. Moosie had wandered back into

steerage to see us and had fallen asleep across our seats, so we crouched together in the aisle. It had been this way all along – as Moosie grew, Nick and I shrank.

At passport control in Vancouver airport, the border guard looked carefully at our son's passport. Then he looked at mine and Nick's, and back at Moosie's again. I waited for his challenge, but it didn't come. This was a country that knew about moose. My mood picked up at once. We were making the right decision, for all of us.

As we trudged to the rental car desk with our backpacks, Moosie's head swung this way and that, taking in all the new sights. He became so excited at the window displays filled with soft toy moose babies that we bought him one. He tucked it tenderly into his bum bag.

Eight hours later, I turned to look at Lucas Imogen Rudolph. He was crammed into the back seat of the tiny rental car. The hard bony branches of his half-grown antlers scraped the roof, and his nose was laid tenderly up against his new cuddly toy. I kept my eyes peeled for movement beside the highway and saw a deer or two hidden in the trees. Other than that, we saw only vast tracts of landscape – lakes and foothills, and later, great purple mountains, rising thousands of metres into the sky, jagged and wonderful and strange.

Moosie was oddly silent. Once or twice we had to stop to pull his antlers out from under the headrest when they got stuck, but the rest of the time he slept. We hadn't really talked about the reason for the trip. The time and the place would do the talking for us. Moosie needed a mate and a bigger back garden, and this was the best way we could think of to make him happy.

"How much longer?" We had been driving for nearly twelve hours on top of the long flight, and we all felt pretty strung out. I longed to stretch my legs, lie down and sleep.

"Almost there," Nick said. He held the map for me to see, his thumb and index finger showing me how close we were to our destination.

chapter 9

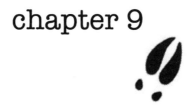

The cabin looked exactly as it had on the web page. It was made of logs, snug and solid, with a huge pile of wood for burning stacked in a shed at the side. Inside, it was decorated with Native American rugs, basic pine furniture and thick woollen blankets folded up on the beds. Everything was a little dusty and smelled of damp and mouse pee. The cabin was a day's drive from just about any place you'd ever want to go, so I guess it wasn't rented very often.

We piled wood into the big iron stove and started a fire, which heated the water and took the chill off the place. Moosie galloped in one door and out the other in a state of high excitement. He bucked and stomped and made little happy whinnying noises, barely able to contain his joy. When we sent him out to explore, he didn't come back for hours.

"It's the right thing we're doing," I murmured to Nick that night. We were tucked up in our bunk beds. "And not just for us. *For him.* Look how happy he is here. He's not too big here, or too clumsy."

"Who'll make his breakfast and help him load his iPod?" Nick's voice was heavy with sadness. "He loves Legoland. I never took him to see the Changing of the Guard at Buckingham Palace."

"He'll be back all the time to visit," I said. But I knew it wasn't true.

chapter 10

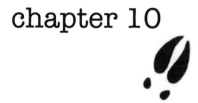

I woke next morning to the smell of bacon and eggs and fresh coffee. Nick had been up since dawn, exploring the surrounding woods. He sounded just like a kid himself.

"The pines are gigantic," he called, "and I saw a beaver! There's a beautiful lake just below here. Come see – and we've got a canoe. The note from the rental agent says it comes with the house. Look at the sky, Jess! We don't have that much blue in all of England."

I was feeling a little blue myself, and it took a hell of an effort to force myself out of bed. Of course I wanted to see all the cool stuff Nick was talking about, but part of me couldn't quite face the day. We were liars and cheats, and poor Moosie thought we were just taking him on holiday, like any loving parents. At last I climbed down from the top bunk and tried to fake a cheerful smile. Nick seemed so happy that I wondered if I'd have to leave him behind, too.

All that day we canoed and lay in the sun while Moosie set off on longer and longer missions to explore the place. At first he'd wander off for half an hour and then bound back to be near us, or to munch twigs in the shade of a tree. He waded into the lake and stood still for a long time, his nose just touching the water. But next time he set off it was hours before he returned. Then before we knew it, the sun had set, and we hadn't seen him since lunchtime.

"Do you think he's OK?" Nick looked gutted.

I nodded.

"What about predators?"

"What predators?"

"Mountain lions. Bears. Eagles."

"Eagles?"

Nick frowned. "Remember that programme where great bloody eagles swooped down from the sky and pecked out people's eyeballs?"

"That was vultures," I said. "Anyway, he'll be fine. He's a big boy now." 'Too big for an eagle to fly off with, Nick, you muppet,' I thought. But I understood his worry. Maybe this was it. Maybe we'd never see our boy again. I felt a strange mixture of sorrow and excitement. So much life lay ahead of him. And us.

By midnight he still wasn't back. Nick and I lay together, awake, straining to hear sounds in the vast woodland. Nature had never seemed so dark and terrifying as it did that night, tempting Moosie into its deepest heart and keeping him there with the promise of freedom. It was only the likes of us who didn't belong here. We felt guilty, like trespassers. Then we thought of Moosie, who had been a sort of trespasser to our way of life all along.

"Do you suppose he's found some sort of den to sleep in?" Nick asked.

"I don't think moose make dens," I said. You'd think Moosie's own father might have looked up 'Moose' on Wikipedia in the three years since he was born.

Nick paused. "Maybe he's found someone to sleep with?"

Whether your son is an 18-year-old couch potato or a three-year-old moose doesn't much matter when it comes to the subject of sex. I couldn't bring myself to think of my velvet baby rutting away with some local townie tart of a moose girl. But that's what all this was about.

And who was I to talk, anyway?

chapter 11

The trip back was quiet. As the big new 757 taxied for take-off, Nick and I held hands, shed a few tears and shivered a little in our crate in the hold. Life never turned out as you expected – we'd certainly learned that lesson.

Moosie and Missy were in first class. We'd had to max out on Nick's parents' credit card just for that. We could imagine them, snorting their love for each other over smoked salmon sandwiches and fancy hand cream.

We agreed that Moosie's girlfriend seemed nice. She had long legs, thick lashes and a wide, friendly mouth. I'd never seen Moosie look so happy and I hoped she wasn't just using him to get her EU passport.

But like I said, life never stops surprising you. A few weeks later, Missy announced that she was pregnant. Mum thought it was hilarious that I was going to be a grandma before my twenty-first birthday. But after the initial shock, I actually began to fancy the idea of a little pink grand-baby with a button nose and no underarm hair. In terms of the genetics, the doctors agreed it was a perfectly likely outcome.

And boy, wouldn't I just love to see the look on their big moosey mugs eight months from now, if a human baby dropped out.

The last laugh was still up for grabs.

Our books are tested
for children and young people by
children and young people.

Thanks to everyone who consulted on
a manuscript for their time and effort in
helping us to make our books better
for our readers.

*More books for **Girls**...*

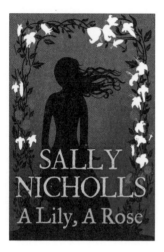

A Lily, A Rose
SALLY NICHOLLS

Elinor has fallen in love for the first time, with Dan, her cousin and knight-in-training.

But her father has other plans. She must marry his friend, Sir William of Courtney – and he's nearly 50!

Can she change her father's mind? And will she ever get to marry Dan?

Wrong Number
CHLOË RAYBAN

It's Saturday night. Marie should be out on a hot date. Or on the town with the girls. Not stuck in front of the telly.

But then the phone rings. It's a wrong number. A hot boy.

Could this be the call Marie has been waiting for?

Wild Song

JANE EAGLAND

Anna's lived on the island all her life. She knows no one else, apart from her father, her father's assistant and two faithful servants.

But one day a strange boy is washed up on the shore. He's wild and free. And he has the power to change everything...

The New Girl

MARY HOOPER

When Kirsty falls out with Bethan, new girl Carly steps in.

Kirsty thinks she's great. But then Carly starts to copy her. At first it's just the odd outfit or hairstyle. Then it starts to get weird.

Things just don't add up. Can Kirsty find out the truth?

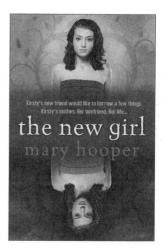

www.barringtonstoke.co.uk